PAGE 10

STORY OF A PAGE

KANHAIYA K

Contents

Prologue   *v*

  1. Came Across   1

  2. Spectre Of Last Night   6

  3. Birds In The Air   12

  4. Lost In Love   17

Day Of Melancholy   25

Prologue

The book is 2nd one from the author. This books inspired from the page 10 of the earlier book named 'Girl with the twisted tattoo" of the author. Author wrote this story after some of the readers feedback to write. Hence the result of that feedback is finally here. This book contains a different story but with the same genre as in page 10 of the earlier book.

Story revolves around the protagonist's activity during a weekend. Story is packed with a grippling events that unfolded as it moves forwards. Author, however tried it; not to deviate from the plot of the story and expecting that readers will get the same content as their feedback.

CHAPTER ONE

Came Across

It was a Thursday evening of Delhi in the mid-summer, you know the climate of Delhi, heat was on its extreme, Viaks was sitting at a planter in the crowded area of Nehru Place just at the exit of metro station, pondering over something and seemed to be lost in that or just relaxing as he was a man of cool nature, who forget anything unpleasant readily and that evening he was frustrated with the office politics and work culture, so he was relaxing over there.

Hi! Came in a voice of foreign girl. Viaks turned towards and responded hi!

It was a very nice and cute girl with her three friends; sitting at the same planter just besides Viaks. Viaks very calmly asked Yes Please!

She, without thinking a minute asked name from Viaks,

She: - Your name please?

Viaks: - It's Viaks.

She: - Nice!

Viaks: - May I know yours please?

She: - Sure! It's Yu-jin!

Viaks: - Very Nice!

Later Yu-jin introduced her friends to Viaks! They are all from Korea.

Viaks reluctantly showed some interest in her friends.

Yu-jin, started asking about Viaks, like what you do, where you live etc., Viaks taken aback, what the fuck, just saw each-other and she intruding in his life. But what could Viaks do, except replying her questions.

He realised that she was taking interest in him or felt that she was just trying to become familiar as seems with her attitude and get relaxed to talk to locals, so Viaks started responding at ease.

Conversation among them getting interesting and so now Viaks was also involved in the gossips, they are willing to know about the Delhi and Viaks was interested or feeling proud to explain good thing about his own country to a foreigner like an expert guide. Yu-jin was impressed with Viaks's nobleness and straightness in attitude while talking. They soon became friends and engulfed in gossips sitting over the same planter, it was already 10 PM, but no one bothering the time they are so involved in each other.

Yu-jin enquired about the nearby Bar from Viaks and expecting to join Viaks as well.

Being local Viaks suggested some of the best bar nearby.

Yu-jin Confirmed for a bar at a kilometre and everyone nodded in agreement Including Viaks.

So, they book an Ola cab and reached the Bar at -Greater Kailash M-block one of the posh area in South Delhi. It was already 10.30 PM and full moon peeping from a bright sky. All they checked in the Bar, named hangout café.

As soon as they entered, a bar tender came for their welcome, Viaks shocked seeing the warm welcome being provided to them. But he readily understand that it was just for the Yu-jin and her friends. She also impressed by the welcome provided to them and thanked Viaks for suggesting that bar.

Viaks was nervous about the next proceeding, what should he order, as it was his first experience with foreigners, so he thought to keep quiet and ask others for their preferences , Yu-jin; beer without thinking a second and thus all agreed on the chilled beer; being it a hot summer, the choice was quite ok.

Deepak, a smartly dressed waiter, jotted it down in his order book, all what they have ordered whether it is beer or other food items like Greek salad, Italian chicken slices etc. Within 15 minutes, their order were on the table and ready for serving. Deepak put a tower of chilled beer and guide them to pour in the glass. They were enjoying each-others company. It was ok for Korean man & women but this was totally new experience for Viaks, who had never drink or even sit with any of the foreigners, which could be sensed from his body language but he was smart enough to hide his weird trait. Being drunk none of his companion noticed him. All the drama ended at 1 AM, when bar tender asked them to closing the bar as per Govt guideline, it cannot be opened beyond the 1AM. Yu-jin asked for bill and Deepak presented it, Yu-jin pulled her purse for payment, but Viaks stopped her and gave his credit card to Deepak. Deepak swapped and returned the card to him.

Now, it's already 1 AM, Yu-jin asked Viaks, where you lived; He replied affirmatively Faridabad, bordering city of Delhi. Viaks asked Yu-jin about her hotel. She said, just at walking distance at Great Park Hotel.

She insisted him to stay with them over night, as it's too late to go bordering city. Her friends also insisted; eventually Viaks agreed. Thus all go on foot to the hotel. Walking 15 minute, they all reached the hotel. They have three rooms for her and her friends and so Yu-jin without delaying a second asked Viaks to come with her. This was what Viaks wants and thus saying good night to all her friends he accompanied Yu-jin to her room.

As soon as gate shut, Yu-jin hugged Viaks with tight grip and started kissing madly, Viaks however, pushing her but Yu-jin was not in mood to leave, and eventually Viaks started responding and inserted his tongue to Yu-jin. Viaks slides his hands towards the back of Yu-jin, and unzipped the dark brown tops of her. She now started moaning; Viaks took her on his hands wrapping her front part with his body. Now both of them engulfed in the sex; all this standing fantasy was continued to some 15 minutes, Viaks then lift her in his lap and put at the bed. She was now completely naked lying at the bed and offering her to Viaks to quench her lust. She clamouring the name of Viaks madly, Viaks went towards the bar area inside the room and picked a luxury Russian Vodka, made two peg of that one for her and other for him. Both seeped it in single shot. By now Viaks also put off his clothes. Seeping a shot of vodka Yu-jin lying at bed and asking for more of her lust. Viaks pour another shot of vodka in a glass and pour it all over the body of her. By now, she was extremely demanding and so Viaks without waiting a minute started kissing her full body starting from her feet. She was now in heaven; moaning extremely in lust like, Viaks, playing with body like a skilled playboy, his sliding tongue now reached at the vaginal part of her, this made her clamouring and sensuous. Both of them giving their full to their fantasy; Yu-jin now gripped his head with her both hand and put at her vagina with full force, as much as she could. Viaks moved to the upper the part of her body and started playing around her navel, this ached her from the waist over the bed by some six inches, Viaks put his hand under the same, started his speed of sipping vodka lying around her navel. He moved to her breast, till now her nipple and breast became hard like any solid things. He started muzzling her nipple with his both hand, he never cared for her moaning, it was full of milk, he was seeping it very madly like a thirsty ox. Yu-jin, squashing Viaks's head moaning very badly, but Viaks not in the mood of let her go. Now Yu-jin took charge of him and put him under her and she was over the Viaks. She, took a bottle of whisky and spread all over the body of Viaks, and Jumped over him and started sucking his cock. Now Viaks's turn to clamour and moan and so it was started. Yu-jin taking full charge of him, teasing him saying you have showed me your way of fantasy now it my turn. Sucking his cock for some 10 minutes, she moved and started kissing with lip lock very badly, Viaks also squashing her boobs and squeezing milk from her milky breast. By now, both were discharged twice but their energy level was still at best. Yu-jin ramming down her body to Viaks's, now jumped on his cock and put her vagina in it, started making shots as madly as she could. Now both were moaning so loudly that anyone crossing lobby near her room must be hearing the noise, or even they were forced to become sensuous. This position last for 10 minutes and now Viaks bend her down on Couch in doggy style and inserted his cock from behind, taking one of her leg in his own hand, as soon as , he inserted his dick , a simple sensual voice of her came out. Viaks was showing no mercy on her and making stroke as speedy as he could, this made her literally crying but she didn't surrender, the fantasy of both were at its extreme. Both were changed position and Yu-jin lying flat at bed, Viaks stroking over her, now they seemed to be exhausted and culminated. Both were laid flat at bed now looking over the roof and felt relaxed.

CHAPTER TWO

Spectre of last Night

It was already 9 in the morning, both were still laid nude on the bed. Viaks got up from the bed, watched time its 9 AM, the office time, but he was relaxed seeing her face in sleep, may be pondering over the night adventure. Then he tried to awake Yu-jin but she was still in deep sleep. He went to washroom to get refreshed. He again tried to awake her, she responded reluctantly and pick his hand, while he was trying to get up from the bed. But, It was already 9.30, He was getting late for office. So, he decided let her sleep and made a note and kept it at nearby bedtable. He then, left room and checked her friends they were not in the room. They were downstairs in the hotel for breakfast, Viaks greeted them Hi, and they responded the same. Then, they were asking about Yu-jin, Viaks said she was still sleeping, he decided to let her sleep. Viaks left the hotel bidding good bye to them.

It was Sharp 10, Viaks, however reached office on time. Everything was going as usual like other day. He went straight to her seat, taking a coffee in hand and wish good morning to all in the department, especially the girl present in the department. She smiled and Viaks so smiled in response. Mobile rang and it was Yu-jin on the other side.

Yu-jin; - Hi, Good morning!

Viaks; - Hi, Very Good Morning!

Yu-jin;- You are quite a good man!

Viaks;- No no its just ok.

Yu-jin;- What's your plan for tonight.

Viaks;- Excitedly nothing much!

Yu-jin; - Then, can you see me in evening.

Viaks; - Why not?

Yu-jin; - Ok. Done!

Viaks; - Ok, bye!

Till now he was relaxed and nothing in his mind about the Yu-jin, but now, after her call and invitation, it was quite a different. Viaks's heart wrenching and its beat could be heard quite a distance of one foot. He was felt excited, which was quite visible from his face. He was now thinking about the last night and how her face, her eye, her hair everything hovering in his mind. No work nothing going well. How could he be relaxed and work while her heart was somewhere? He was in completely fell in love with Yu-jin. Here the gentleman fell in love, from which he was on run. Now he was waiting for evening only.

His boss Mr. Ravindra called Viaks,

Viaks; - Coming to his senses, said yes sir!

Ravindra:- Where are you?

Viaks;- Very calmly, here sir!

Ravindra;- It doesn't seem so.

How Ravindra would know about her mental condition?

Viaks;- stammering no no sir!

Ravindra: - Then, where was the fortnightly report you are supposed to be presented to me.

Viaks; - Oh sorry! Just forgot the same. I'll provide you within an hour.

(It was supposed to happen in love; Viaks in mind)

Ravindra; - Prioritize your work Mr Vikkie!

Viaks went straight to his seat and opened his Laptop now for work after reminder! He opened his laptop but his mind not in his control, then how to make report, all data he required need to collect from other department as well. Anyway he was started doing his work, forgetting her, but he was not able to connect the dots required to make because of lost concentration. He was lucky, his boss has to go outside from office due to some work, so he got all day to work upon without any disturbance; eventually he had done his work and mailed to his boss but not earlier than 4PM. As soon as he mailed his report, he subsequently WhatsApp his boss for short leave. As a good gesture or could say by his luck, it was approved by his boss.

As soon leave approved, he rushed to nearby metro station and board to his house as he has to change his clothes and need to return by 6 PM at the designated place. In between both were chatting about plan, Here Viaks was aggressively eager to meet again. Viaks reached his house and changed his clothes and put a set of extra in his bag, as he was planning for 1 more days.

Here Yu-jin was waiting for him, her friends already flew for Korea in the morning itself Yu-jin stayed here for some more days. Viaks reached at the place where Yu-jin was already waiting.

Viaks: - Sorry Sorry! Hope you have not to wait much!

Yu-jin: - It's ok. Not much.

Yu-jin: - So, what's the plan? What we are going to roam around.

Viaks; - What do you likemost, what is your area of interest I'll make the plan accordingly.

Yu-jin; - ok. Lemme think! I would like to see heritage of Delhi, for which it is quite famous.

Viaks: - Ok, then! However the list is too long, can't be covered in a single day, that's too in evening not good idea. We need at least 2 full day to cover this.

Yu-jin; - Ok, I am fine with that let's start our journey

Viaks;- Today, we'll go the India Gate, as it's already 7 PM here, India gate is nice place to hang out in open.

Yu-jin; - Yup!

They booked a cab for India Gate from Nehru Place, its showing 15 min. waiting time. In Delhi, online cab facility arrived some 5 year ago but still in peak hour waiting time is 15 to 30 min.

Viaks;- In korea also, this kind of waiting problem in vogue.

Yu-jin;- No no! 2 to 3 Min is enough.

Viaks;- Wow good! Enjoy the Indian online taxi service too!

Viaks;- Where's your friend today?

Yu-jin;- They all were left to Seol.

Viaks;- What ! And you are here, why?

Yu-jin;- They were not my friend, but we met at airport and so, we accompanied each-other on this trip. They were students, came here on study trip, and yesterday was their last day over here from their university, so they have gone.

Viaks;- And what's your purpose over here.

Yu-jin:- I just came here for tour, as I am freelance vlogger and wishing to explore India for its heritage and make vlog on that.

Viaks: - That's good! You will get too much content for your vlog here in Delhi only, leave India.

Cab arrived to the booked point, both were sit in and cab driver move towards the destination, after confirming OTP from the bookie.

It was Friday evening, it was also too hot outside, inside taxi they got relaxed somehow. Anyway they reached India Gate and fare got deducted from the wallet of Viaks. It was almost 8 PM ;(its time not whisky) by reaching over there, still there were too much of crowd. Yu-jin excited seeing the lighting and decoration over there. India Gate is a good place for night owls, as there are whole night people especially bachelors roaming around. Viaks took her to an Ice cream counter, as she was screamed for ice-cream. Finishing Ice-cream she took out her camera and started clicking picture of the India Gate and scenery around. She asked him to sit around India Gate and took out his picture and then Viaks took hers. Both were enjoying the night with full of energy, taking picture, making vlog, enjoying street food at Rajpath.

It was really an awesome experience for her and him as well. Living in Delhi for last 10 years, Viaks never enjoyed so much but that night was special. Why it not special would for him, as one of the beautiful girl, was accompanying him. It was almost 2 AM in the morning, Viaks asked her to go the hotel, But Yu-jin was reluctant; as she was not let the night go, but Viaks now felt tired, because of sleep.

Yu-jin also observed it that now it's not possible for him to even stand to sleep. She already delayed many time by saying 10 minute. But this time, she agreed and booked taxi, as Viaks was not able to open his eyes. Being it 2.30 AM morning, Cab came immediately, they sit in and cab drove the way , as map on his screen showing, within 20 Minute, anyway cab reached the destination, Yu-jin paid in cash to him, by now Viaks also took a nap in cab, now Viaks felt somehow fresh. Both went upstairs and Yu-jin unlocked the door; as soon as door unlocked, Viaks just went to bed and slept, without even changing.

Yu-jin, came after changing her dress and saw Viaks lied on the bed, so she put a blanket over him, and she slept just besides.

Next day, it was Saturday; the off day for Viaks, so Viaks has no hurry and sleeping besides her, with twisting his arm around the neck of Yu-jin, It was by now clearly evident that both were in love. It's not from the Viaks's side but Yu-jin also responding with same energy and attitude.

CHAPTER THREE

Birds in the Air

Both the love birds are still in bed; involved in cuddling and chuckling but not doing active sex.

Yu-jin, waking up at 10 AM, seeing Viaks still sleeping; kissed him at his cheek and went to bathroom for taking shower. She came, some half an hour later and still saw, he was sleeping, she pinned his nose, while waking him up, He pulled her upon himself but Yu-jin was not in the mood, So, she pushed him and told him to wake up as its almost 10, need to go outside.

Then Yu-jin went down stairs for breakfast.

Hey Viaks! Sitting in cafeteria, Yu-jin, greeted him

Hi Yu-jin! Viaks responded.

Yu-jin; - Finally you woke up! (Laughs)

Viaks; - you have not made me wake up.

Yu-jin; - I tried, but you were slept like 'Bhasmasur' of Hindu mythology's.

Viaks; - No No! Embarrassingly, it was off day and so its routine, which subconscious mind, perceived.

Yu-jin; - So, Mr. What would you take?

Viaks; - Nothing, I'll just take a toast and orange Juice. Viaks asked a waiter for the same.

Both the love birds have taken their breakfast and went outside in lawn for a walk.

Viaks; - So, where do you want to go today?

Yu-jin; - I don't know! Surprisingly, your city and you better know about.

Viaks; - I know that, but you are my guest here, and courteously, I need to ask your wish.

Yu-jin; - ok ok! I already impressed with your hospitality, so no more formality, we are now friends. Let's go somewhere!

Viaks; - Ok then!

They took a cab for red fort, which was going to take some One hour from Nehru place. Both were now really enjoying each-others company, Viaks was in heaven, even can be said that he was totally lost. Being alone for a quite long since his break-up from Pooja.

Anyway he has moved in current relationship. It was not from one side but from the other side too. Cab reached red fort, Viaks thanked driver, which was something unusual from Indian to thank driver, milkwallah etc. but Viaks somehow managed to show Yu-jin, that Indians are also well cultured. He left no situation to impress Yu-jin. Viaks took a ticket for himself and one for foreigner. Yu-jin amazed to see the Crowd at Red Fort, which was one of the main attraction of the city. Viaks, like guide explaining all the thing to her about the Red fort and story behind. Now Viaks was also opened completely and left formality of being courteousness. Yu-jin was clicking pic of every nook and corner, she didn't want to leave anything for her memoir. Now, it became the more attractive, since its taking over by a private player, under a flagship project of the current Govt's heritage monetization Policy. Earlier, it was managed by Govt and so there were less amenities like restrau, entertainment zones etc. but now all this was available. They were now at one of the restaurant inside the

Red Fort.

They were spending quality times with each other, Having lunch they both sat under a tree in the remote corner of the campus, it was sunny day, so the shade of the tree made them relax for a while, Viaks was on the lap of Yu-jin, both were engulfed in the romance, leaving no stone unturned to enjoy every bit of time. Yu-jin, fingering in hair of Viaks, she was asking about Viaks's life past, Viaks told plainly everything about his relationship in past. Yu-jin, also telling them his office affairs, with Mr. Can, but that was short lived relationship, which was lately came to an end, however the decision was taken mutually.

Viaks asked very excitedly, so you are too single now, She said normally yeh! It was already 5 in the evening, both were just roaming around nearby of red fort. The area often called heritage of Delhi. Yu-jin, was very keen to learn about the more n more about Delhi, so that she can make good vlog, which were eventually going to help many her country mate. That's also the reason for her to roam around, enjoying Delhi, Street food of Chandani Chowk, Red fort etc.

Now, it was 7PM in the evening, both decided to go to the nearby Bar, Viaks suggested to go to CP(Connaught Place), the famous downtown area of the city, designed by the Britishers. So, taking auto from the Chandani chowk , both went CP and picked Prime street café to went upstairs, the market was designed such that Bar and restrau was upstairs and on ground floor, rest of the shopping stuff were available.

They sat at the corner point that seems to be couple friendly, music was loud and people were dancing too, Viaks asked her choice for liquor, she glanced at the menu and said Black label, whisky, Viaks never drank such a costly whisky, so, and he somehow shocked but managed to escape the embarrassing situation.

A Bartender came to them and asked how would he serve? Viaks asked his name, attendant told his name Love Kumar, then Viaks asked him for two large whisky of black label and an Italian crispy chicken kabab, with Greek salad.

Love; - Your Whisky Sir!

Viaks; - Thanks! Where's other stuff?

Love; - on way sir!

Viaks; - Okay.

Love came with their other stuff and serve on the table according to their protocol, as it's was date night for the couple. Both the love birds were enjoying the dinner date. Yu-jin was admiring the choice of Viaks and bar as well. The admiring word from Yu-jin, making Viaks confident and at the same time he also felt some unease, thinking it might be false admiration. But whatever it might be, Viaks was liking her. The romantic dinner date end at the bar and both came outside in fresh air, it was 11 in the night. Now where to go, Yu-jin asked him, he simply replied, where do you want? Yu-jin, replied, it's your city, take me where, you want. Viaks pondering over the situation, while strolling at the street of CP in almost midnight. Booze were now showing effect on both of them, as theirs legs were faltering. Seeing this, Viaks thought it would be better to go to hotel, where Yu-jin stays, so, he booked a cab.

Cab arrived some 10 minute later, till now both were keep strolling at the street nearby. Cab arrived and took them to hotel just within 25 minute from CP to NP. Being midnight, there were no traffic, all the road were smooth. It was Viaks's 3rd night only with Yu-jin, but seeing both, it didn't seem so, rather it seemed that both were friends since long.

Viaks opened the door, both were heavily drunk and entered with hand in hand. Viaks shut the door, as door shut, Viaks lift Yu-jin in his lap and started kissing, for which he was waited since day long. Yu-jin was also responding his call. Kissing some ten minutes at standing, Viaks put her on Couch, then licking her lips, it's too hot to handle, for Viaks. He started undressing her, put her tops and jeans off. She was in just a bra and panty lying at Couch. He was licking her navel, she started screaming and moaning loudly, but Viaks was not caring, increased his speed of licking her whole body. By now he was undressed too. Yu-jin, took the charge and came upon the Viaks and started sucking his cock, this simmers Viaks from inside, and Yu-jin was at her peak. He was moaning, squashing her head to her dick. Viaks took Yu-jin from hair and bring her to his mouth. Again they were lip-locking, kissing intensely, looks like they were eating each other. Viaks, now put her on bed and started stroking her, she again started screaming loudly, he increased his speed of stroking, and they were completely lost in lust.

CHAPTER FOUR

Lost in Love

Still weekend was left for a day, so the one full day left for Viaks to romance with her. As it was Sunday next day, so both were sleeping late in the morning or why not they'll sleep late after what adventure they had done the whole night. It seems that nothing left in theirs life except romance or sex. Its 8 AM, still they were lying in bed full nude with crossed arm with each other, cuddling, chucking and romancing.

Viaks didn't want to leave her for a second, not only Viaks but Yu-jin too, they were so engrossed in love and lust.

Yu-jin; - what's the plan of today?

Viaks; - I just want to see you whole day.

Yu-jin blushed at!

Viaks; - Smiled and pinch her nose! Laughs!

Yu-jin; - Ok then, let's see! How long can you see me?

Now Viaks blushed and laughs!

Viaks no no, I mean to be with you, where only you and I were present.

Yu-jin; - ok ok, obviously I would be with you. I also want the same. In fact I love to be with you.

Viaks; - I know, I think, how would I live, when you would go to your country!

Yu-jin; - Can come with me, I'll will be waiting for you!

Viaks; - kissed the forehead of Yu-jin and said, we would be together forever.

Yu-jin; - nodded and planted a kiss on his cheek.

Viaks; - would you like to visit my home, where I am living alone.

Yu-jin; - why not?

Viaks: - Ok, todays night will be spent at my home.

Yu-jin;- Ok. Done!

(Both were laughing and chuckles)

Yu-jin got up from the bed, planting a kiss on Viaks and went to take shower. Meanwhile Viaks, slept again, till she came from shower. She came, seeing he was on deep sleep.

Hey! Viaks

Viaks in sleepy mood, what!

Its 11, get up, we need to go out for some shopping- Yu-jin reminded him.

Viaks; - What the fuck! (In minds, without mincing a word). But in word he said, Oh Sorry Sorry! Wait for a minute.

Viaks was contemplating, today, my credit card going to be bust, But what could he do, it's the by-product of love, comes with. So he had to face the situation.

He got up and went straight to washroom, came some 30 minute later.

Here Yu-jin was getting angry on his lackadaisical attitude, so as soon as Viaks came from washroom, she screamed over; what the fuck you are doing, Viaks, you are not bothering the time. I have to shop many things, will be late.

Viaks, however prepared for this kind of slur from a girl, as, it was normal for him. He told her, just wait outside at the cafeteria and order for one coffee for me and anything you like for yours. I'll be there within minute.

After a while, Viaks went down to cafeteria.

Viaks; - Hi sweetheart!

Yu-jin; - Hi, with sad mood!

Viaks; - Sorry dear! Will enjoy a lot today! Don't worry, just finish your juice..

Yu-jin; - Ok! Smiles!

Viaks; - As usual, fell on this smile!

Both finishing their coffee, put their glass at the table and smiled at each other, exited with hand in gloves, as if both were in deep love, in fact, it seems so, by seeing their attitude. But only time will tell, which would be, when she goes to her native country.

Both went to select city walk, a high end mall in South Delhi. This time both were enjoying the ride of Delhi Metro, from Nehru Enclave to Saket. She was impressed upon the service provided by the DMRC and its maintenance. Viaks was also happy, listening admiration for his country, he also add some masala in it.

They entered the high end mall, like a close knitted couple, Yu-jin was so happy but Viaks was not, as his pocket going to lose. It's not easy for anyone to make shopping for his girlfriend in a high end mall.

It was her 10th store, which she was visiting, still she had not purchased any single unit of clothes, here Viaks was now tired of that, but not reflecting so, just taking her clothes in hand as she was trying one after another, at last she picked two, Viaks pursed out to pay the bill, Yu-jin stopped him from paying so, saying I'll pay for it, why are you paying? Viaks said no no just like that, here in our culture, when a male and female went for shopping, generally male pay for the expenditure, as his duty. Yu-jin, what the fuck man, you people are making lady humiliate by doing so, let her to shop own her own. So, it's my shopping and I'll pay for it. Viaks, taking long breathe, said okay. Yu-jin paid the bill of INR 18000.

After shopping, they went to pizza shop and ordered one large crispy onion pizza with extra cheez on it and two thumps up of 250 ml each. Till the order arrive, Yu-jin was sitting at the table, looking at Viaks with love, Viaks sensed it and blushed at. No one seen him like that till now. It was not his fault for being single from quite a long time, but it's his nature of being open to all, what he feel he said in front of anyone. He speaks from his heart not from his mind unlike others in this world.

Yu-jin, being foreigners and came from highly modernised country, she sensed Viaks's nature and fell in love with him. Order bell rang no 49, which was for them, so Viaks went to the counter to pick that and came with the order.Yes, this time Viaks paid the bill. Both were feeling hungry, as it was 3 of the afternoon without food. Eating Pizza, Viaks proposed her for a movie, and Yu-jin said ok without thinking for a second. But asked, which movie, and suggest any SRK Films available in the theatre, as being a huge fan for SRK. Luckily, there were a SRK Movie 'Jab Tak Hai Jaan' was released this weekend, a romantic film produced under YRF banner. It was in Hindi, Viaks said her, she replied excitedly no problem, I know some Hindi, I can understand and observe, whenever I felt you'll help me to get that point. Now Viaks's role was going to be a translator for her. This is love, anything can be done, if possible for human being.

Now the show was from 5 PM, they had finished their Pizza by then and went straight to the cinema floor, both took the ticket from the counter and entre the area, it was Audi 3. Seat no was in H row 17 and 18. It was still 5 minute remaining to start the film, meanwhile people were taking their respective seats, and ad was running on the screen.

It was huge clamour inside the theatre, which was quite understandable for the Indians, but a foreigner, who was not experienced any such event would be Primafacei shocked; so Yu-jin, was!

Yu-jin; - Why was this noise Viaks.

Viaks; - Replied politely, its SRK entry dear, his fans are over here. It's a welcome for SRK in each theatre. Just experience and enjoy.

Yu-jin; - Omg! This welcome for a movie star in a theatre! Totally shocked Yu-jin!

Viaks; - Yeh! Yu-jin!

Somehow film finished in crowdy environment!

Exiting from the theatre, Yu-jin, was so happy explaining it to Viaks, A SRK movie, that's also in India, among his local fans, it was quite a life time experience for her.

They took metro to avoid the Delhi's Traffic, which might take some extra minute, but surely save them from the sluggishness of taxi in heavy traffic. It took them to almost one and half hour to reach Faridabad, from where, Viaks book taxi for 15 Minute drive to sector 88, which falls under the Greater Faridabad.

On 12th Floor, Viaks opened the door and welcome her in a very romantic voice, she responded. He showed her, his 1bhk apartment as if she was already her newly married wife. She was also responding positively. Standing at balcony, she felt relaxed from the nuisance of the city. The apartment was at the newly developed area at the outskirts of the city, some 5 KM away from the stir of the main city. Being part of the NCR, city was already developed and still in making one of the smart city of the country, as announced by the current Govt. So, Viaks, standing just besides her at the balcony, seeing open sky with full of stars and glittering, one moon in sky and other besides him, feeling romantic. Gossiping some 15 minutes enjoying the open sky from the balcony, asked her for her choice for the dinner. She asked for some light food, so Viaks ordered the same from Zomato, the new start up food delivery app in the country. It will take some half an hour to arrive and in the meantime Viaks brought up two glass of Russian Vodka one for each other. Viaks, wanted to feel the every moment of this romantic night; knowing that then when will such kind of thing would happen in his life.

Doorbell rang, Viaks opened the door, it was his order, Viaks took the order and gave Rs 50 to the delivery boy as tip, which was not usual for Viaks, he never felt this to give tip but today they felt it. He Put the stuff in the kitchen and went to balcony to finish the remaining stuff in glass with his love. Both of them, finished the whisky and came to dining table, Viaks pulled the chair and made way for Yu-jin, asking to sit. Yu-jin, thanked him for his romantic gesture. Viaks put the light off and burned the candle and sodium light that filled the atmosphere with romance.

Yu-jin was surprised, seeing all this and asked Viaks, when could you planned all this? Which was quite surprising as, since last two days Viaks was with her.

Viaks replied, Just planned, everything was available at my home, so just clicked in my mind and I executed.

Yu-jin thanked!

Viaks urged not to thank him, it was just his pleasure to host her. Both smiled romantically.

Now, what the food stuff was, Viaks order some tasty local cuisine in non veg, it was Afgani chicken, Chicken Tandoori rara and Roomali roti. Viaks put all the stuff at the table with a bottle of Russian Vodka.

He poured the vodka in glass for each other and cheers for their new relationship, It was not usual for Yu-jin as well. She never expected that she would find an Indian boy and date him like that. But it was Viaks, who proved her wrong. Both were enjoying the dinner and date as well, gazing each other in eye. Finishing dinner, both were sat at the nearby couch with vodka in hand. Both were sitting in arm twisting way, Viaks fingering her hair, kissing her neck, forehead. By now, both were ready to immerse in each other and Vodka also started its magic. Both were now wrapped up in each other and romancing the night with glamour of love, candle light dinner, vodka and they are going to lust as well.

Viaks kissed her on forehead with his finger in her hair and admiring her for her cuteness and beauty. Listening all this, Yu-jin, lost herself in the arm of Viaks and planted a kiss on his lips. Viaks instantly responded and picked her lips. Both were now lip locking each other. They were now totally engrossed in the love. Viaks slightly down his tongue to her neck and squeezing her from behind. She started moaning slowly and responding with Viaks's move as if both were made for each other. She started removing Viaks's clothes and Viaks do the same for her. He dropped her clothes there and picked her juicy boobs, squashing boobs from here & there. She were also trying to put her all boobs in Viaks's mouth. Viaks was sucking and squeezing it wildly. She was now moaning loudly, it's her turn to take the move and so she came up and started playing with the solid body of the Viaks. She were sucking his chest, nipple and core, after playing some time with his body, she moved up and kissed his cheek and squeezing his head. As soon she squeezed his head, he picked her from hair and pulled her towards him and put his tongue in her mouth. Now, again both were licking each-others mouth wildly. He was also pressing her boobs in between. This lip locking continues for some ten minutes. Viaks put off her kalvin klien panty and laid down her in doggy style and put her boner from behind. Stroking madly without bothering her clamour and cry. She was just helpless now, Viaks was in no mood to let her go without satisfying his lust. Now, he laid her flat on the couch and inserted his boner like iron rod in her pink pussy and started stroking, she again started moaning and squeezing him from back and pulling him towards her. She was now took her cock in her mouth and started sucking it like a juicy mango, saliva from her lips were draining out. Viaks was pushing her head on his dick so that she could swallow all over across the throat and so in between she coughed from many a times, as she took all the cock to her throat. Viaks, now took her in lap and kissing all, the where he could and she responded the same in amateur. He put her on the bed in flat position and penetrate his boner through the wet pussy, which was now became red rose after spending so much time in sex. She cried and soon he entered his rock solid dick but as the stroke passed, she started enjoying the stroke and moaning. It was so intense that she was aching over waist again & again. She came over Viaks and started riding his cock, Viaks was lying down at the bed and just feeling the sex. As Viaks was now to cum and so pushed her and spread all his sperm all over around her navel. Now, relaxed both were just lie down besides each other without mincing a word but a romantic kiss in her forehead.

Day Of Melancholy

In the morning, Yu-jin had return flight from IGI, so they had to wake up early. Viaks reluctantly wanted to go but he was a different kind of person, who take love in other way not as in general people take. He believe, love is the thing that makes people free and it's a feeling not the restriction or possession. So, while Yu-jin was getting prepared for her trip to her native country, Viaks was just seeing her.

Yu-jin;- Viaks get up! I am going to be late.

Viaks;- Oh no! You'll be on time darling!

Yu-jin;- It's already 6 and flight is at 10.

Viaks; - Ok. Have you done your packing?

Yu-jin;- Yeh! It's almost done.

Viaks;- Will leave this place at 6.30 sharp! (Pinch her cheek.)

Viaks booked a taxi, being it morning, less no of taxi is available, so it will take time. In between, Viaks get readied, by then taxi also came to the apartment. Both boarded the taxi and left for Airport.

The love weekend had been ended and the time for their departure from the heaven, which would not going to be easy at least for Viaks. Taxi driver was taking its route via google map and both the love birds were busy in romantic gossips. Yu-jin was admiring Viaks for his hospitality and off course for his sense of humour and love. Viaks was also responding in the same way like Yu-jin's.

Taxi arrived at the airport and driver had to remind both the love birds, as they were engrossed in the romantic gossips. Viaks paid the fare and both were moved towards the entrance of the T3 terminal. The flight was at 10.00 and still there were two hour left for the departure. Viaks now feeling under the heaviness of his heart, as her weekend love really going far from him. Yu-jin was also emotional like Viaks, which was quite normal for anyone. Announcement starts for Flight No T214 for seoul, the same flight Yu-jin had to board, so they were hugged each other and Lyida made her way towards the check-in point. Viaks was seeing her standing still at the same point, till she became out of sight, waving hand in bye.

It was 9 by then and Viaks's office was at 10 at kalkaji, he could not go by road and so take metro from there, which will also going to take one and half hour at least. Anyway that's okay for him.

He reached the office at 10.30 and went to his seat, wishing good morning to everyone. Where he got call from Mr. Ravindra, so, he went to this cabin and asked why did he called him. Ravindra, Viaks, I found some corrections need to be made the report you have sent me on Friday. To discuss that point, I have called you here and Ravindra put the paper, painted in ink before him what would you say about. Look at the thing and correct accordingly, Viaks replied okay Ravindra, I'll take a look and let you inform. Viaks take the paper and came to his seat and started analysing the corrections. Once they got the point they made the necessary corrections and revert to Ravindra. He was cool, as if, nothing happened with him the weekend. The day ended as usual and Viaks's life continues as just before the meeting Yu-jin.

The seven hour flight of Yu-jin landed at Incheon International airport at 5 PM. It took Yu-jin some 30 minute to exit the airport after completing the formality. Viaks was waiting for her call on her landing over there, by now which should be done, this increases his heartbeat, why did she not called yet, so he tried whatsapp call, but she couldn't pick. Again he dialled, this time she picked up.

Yu-jin; - Hi Viaks, How'z the day.

Viaks; - Good! How'z your journey darling!

Yu-jin; - Awesome!

Viaks; - That good!

Yu-jin; - I missed my country so much these days, finally I am here.

Viaks;- off course! Darling! You have missed that, hope, now, you will enjoy the seoul! By the way, what's famous in your country?

Yu-jin;- Nothing much heritage like yours, but certainly some of fine infrastructure like N. Seoul Tower, Lotte world Tower, Blue House etc., what else you would expect from a capitalist country.

Viaks;- Nice; listening your word from seoul, still feeling you are here.

Viaks;- Have you reached home?

Yu-jin;- No not yet, but about to reach.

Viaks;- Ok then, reach home and take rest, as you could be tired of hectic seven hour journey of flight.

Yu-jin; - Yeh Sure! Would connect you later. Bye!

Viaks; Bye!

Everything was quite fine by now but it was not going to be any longer, as soon as Viaks opened door of his apartment, he found all the stuff as it was the last night. This started reminding every event that took place the last night over there. Viaks was drowning in the memoir of last night or even say the weekend. The glass of Vodka, the moon from the balcony, the dining table, couch etc. everything what he saw creates her picture in his eyes. He was getting nervous but he was trying hard to resist this memoir but now the distance of her making him drowsy.

In the morning, Yu-jin had return flight from IGI, so they had to wake up early. Viaks reluctantly wanted to go but he was a different kind of person, who take love in other way not as in general people take. He believe, love is the thing that makes people free and it's a feeling not the restriction or possession. So, while Yu-jin was getting prepared for her trip to her native country, Viaks was just seeing her.

Yu-jin;- Viaks get up! I am going to be late.

Viaks;- Oh no! You'll be on time darling!

Yu-jin;- It's already 6 and flight is at 10.

Viaks; - Ok. Have you done your packing?

Yu-jin;- Yeh! It's almost done.

Viaks;- Will leave this place at 6.30 sharp! (Pinch her cheek.)

Viaks booked a taxi, being it morning, less no of taxi is available, so it will take time. In between, Viaks get readied, by then taxi also came to the apartment. Both boarded the taxi and left for Airport.

The love weekend had been ended and the time for their departure from the heaven, which would not going to be easy at least for Viaks. Taxi driver was taking its route via google map and both the love birds were busy in romantic gossips. Yu-jin was admiring Viaks for his hospitality and off course for his sense of humour and love. Viaks was also responding in the same way like Yu-jin's.

Taxi arrived at the airport and driver had to remind both the love birds, as they were engrossed in the romantic gossips. Viaks paid the fare and both were moved towards the entrance of the T3 terminal. The flight was at 10.00 and still there were two hour left for the departure. Viaks now feeling under the heaviness of his heart, as her weekend love really going far from him. Yu-jin was also emotional like Viaks, which was quite normal for anyone. Announcement starts for Flight No T214 for seoul, the same flight Yu-jin had to board, so they were hugged each other and Lyida made her way towards the check-in point. Viaks was seeing her standing still at the same point, till she became out of sight, waving hand in bye.

It was 9 by then and Viaks's office was at 10 at kalkaji, he could not go by road and so take metro from there, which will also going to take one and half hour at least. Anyway that's okay for him.

He reached the office at 10.30 and went to his seat, wishing good morning to everyone. Where he got call from Mr. Ravindra, so, he went to this cabin and asked why did he called him. Ravindra, Viaks, I found some corrections need to be made the report you have sent me on Friday. To discuss that point, I have called you here and Ravindra put the paper, painted in ink before him what would you say about. Look at the thing and correct accordingly, Viaks replied okay Ravindra, I'll take a look and let you inform. Viaks take the paper and came to his seat and started analysing the corrections. Once they got the point they made the necessary corrections and revert to Ravindra. He was cool, as if, nothing happened with him the weekend. The day ended as usual and Viaks's life continues as just before the meeting Yu-jin.

The seven hour flight of Yu-jin landed at Incheon International airport at 5 PM. It took Yu-jin some 30 minute to exit the airport after completing the formality. Viaks was waiting for her call on her landing over there, by now which should be done, this increases his heartbeat, why did she not called yet, so he tried whatsapp call, but she couldn't pick. Again he dialled, this time she picked up.

Yu-jin; - Hi Viaks, How'z the day.

Viaks; - Good! How'z your journey darling!

Yu-jin; - Awesome!

Viaks; - That good!

Yu-jin; - I missed my country so much these days, finally I am here.

Viaks;- off course! Darling! You have missed that, hope, now, you will enjoy the seoul! By the way, what's famous in your country?

Yu-jin;- Nothing much heritage like yours, but certainly some of fine infrastructure like N. Seoul Tower, Lotte world Tower, Blue House etc., what else you would expect from a capitalist country.

Viaks;- Nice; listening your word from seoul, still feeling you are here.

Viaks;- Have you reached home?

Yu-jin;- No not yet, but about to reach.

Viaks;- Ok then, reach home and take rest, as you could be tired of hectic seven hour journey of flight.

Yu-jin; - Yeh Sure! Would connect you later. Bye!

Viaks; Bye!

Everything was quite fine by now but it was not going to be any longer, as soon as Viaks opened door of his apartment, he found all the stuff as it was the last night. This started reminding every event that took place the last night over there. Viaks was drowning in the memoir of last night or even say the weekend. The glass of Vodka, the moon from the balcony, the dining table, couch etc. everything what he saw creates her picture in his eyes. He was getting nervous but he was trying hard to resist this memoir but now the distance of her making him drowsy.